W9-CZV-684

I GET AROUND
IN MY OWN
SPECIAL WAY

by Donna Goldman
Illustrated by William Morton

Copyright © 2020 by Donna Goldman

All rights reserved. No part of this publication may be reproduced, scanned, uploaded, stored in a retrieval system, or transmitted, in any form or by any means, electronic, mechanical, photocopying, recording, or otherwise, without the prior written permission of the publisher.

This is a work of fiction. Names, characters, places, and incidents either are the product of the author's imagination or are used fictitiously, and any resemblance to an actual person, living or dead, business, companies, events or locales is entirely coincidental.

ISBN: 978-1-0878-5643-8

Published by Whitehall Publishing
Graphic design by Debra Broutman Berk

Contact Donna Goldman at gtbkupthebook@gmail.com.

"For my wonderful family, especially Maia, Tess, Eve, Lauren and Graham. You fill my heart with joy."

-D.G.

I get around in a special way
that lets me **LEARN** and **PLAY** and **SHARE**.
Instead of walking like you can do,
I ride in my wheelchair.

Not a chair like you sit in,
that is TINY or very **TALL**.
That would not help me to get around
in any way at all!

It's a chair with special wheels,
so **I CAN HAVE FUN TIMES WITH YOU**:
Do arts and craft projects, go on sleepovers,
and play sports with my friends —

WHOO HOO!

My legs don't work the same way as yours —
it's hard to skip and run.
But I still like going to the zoo and the park
where I have TONS OF FUN!

I like to **HAVE FUN** and
PLAY WITH MY FRIENDS
and find out what I can do myself,
but sometimes I need a little help
to reach a toy or book on the shelf.

We really are not so different

I think we enjoy the same things —
like **PLAYING** and **PAINTING**
and **BUILDING** with **BLOCKS**
and learning new songs to sing.

I'll bet that you like ICE CREAM like me.

I think sundaes are so delish!

Let's eat some and celebrate — my birthday or yours —

and don't forget to make a wish!

It makes me sad when people look away
or even stop and stare.

I would love a **smile**
or a friendly wave
when you pass me on my chair.

I LIKE TO HELP,
so if you're carrying toys
and can only hold on to three,
I can help you carry the others
by resting them on my knees.

Some people have **GLASSES** to help them see
or **HEARING AIDS** to help them hear;
some wear **BRACES** to straighten their teeth...
and I get around in my wheelchair.

PROSTHETIC LEGS, **SEGWAYS** too, each with **their special touches**.

IF YOU SEE ME in my wheelchair
and wonder if I could use some pushes,
please ask me first if I'd like some help
or we could both land on our *tushes!*

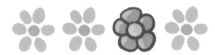

BEING DIFFERENT CAN BE TRICKY,

but I'm tough and I can do it.
If I fall, I get right back up
and that's all there is to it.

I'M PROUD OF ME! If anyone asks, I sit up straight, smile and say, **"I'm just like you, but I happen to get around in my own special way."**